Published by Tuttle Publishing,
an imprint of Periplus Editions (HK) Ltd,
with editorial offices at 364 Innovation Drive,
North Clarendon, VT 05759-9436, USA and
130 Joo Seng Road #06-01, Singapore 368357

Text © 2006 Periplus Editions (HK) Ltd
Illustrations © 2006 Roger Clark
LCC Card No: 2005910618
ISBN 13: 978-0-8048-3645-6
ISBN 10: 0-8048-3645-0

First printing, 2006

Printed in Malaysia

10 09 08 07 06
5 4 3 2 1

TUTTLE PUBLISHING® is a registered trademark of
Tuttle Publishing.

DISTRIBUTED BY:

North America, Latin America & Europe
Tuttle Publishing,
364 Innovation Drive,
North Clarendon, VT 05759-9436, USA
Tel: (802) 773 8930 Fax: (802) 773 6993
Email: info@tuttlepublishing.com
Website: www.tuttlepublishing.com

Asia Pacific
Berkeley Books Pte Ltd,
130 Joo Seng Road #06-01,
Singapore 368357
Tel: (65) 6280 1330 Fax: (65) 6280 6290
Email: inquiries@periplus.com.sg
Website: www.periplus.com

Japan
Tuttle Publishing,
Yaekari Building 3F, 5-4-12 Osaki,
Shinagawa-ku, Tokyo 141-0032
Tel: (03) 5437 0171 Fax: (03) 5437 0755
Email: tuttle-sales@gol.com

Glossary

An **elf** is a small, often mischievous fairy that plays tricks on people.

A **grouch** is a person who is irritable or complains regularly.

A **locket** is a small case that can be opened to hold someone's photo or momento.
It is usually made of gold or silver and worn on a chain around the neck.

Mittens are gloves that cover the four fingers together and the thumb separately.

Konnyaku jelly is a sweet, chewy, semi-transparent usually fruit-filled jelly.
This nutritious Japanese jelly is made of Konnyaku flour, which comes from a root from
the taro family known as Konnyaku.

A **sonnet** is a poem with fixed rhyme pattern. It has 14 lines, of 10 syllables each.

Soya bean milk or **soybean milk** is a nutritious drink, made from ground soya bean and
water. It can be drunk as a milk substitute, and also used in some infant formulas.

What Do You Do With This Book?

Rhyming Fun for Everyone.

TUTTLE PUBLISHING
Tokyo • Rutland, Vermont • Singapore

What do you have on your **back**?

A **sack**.

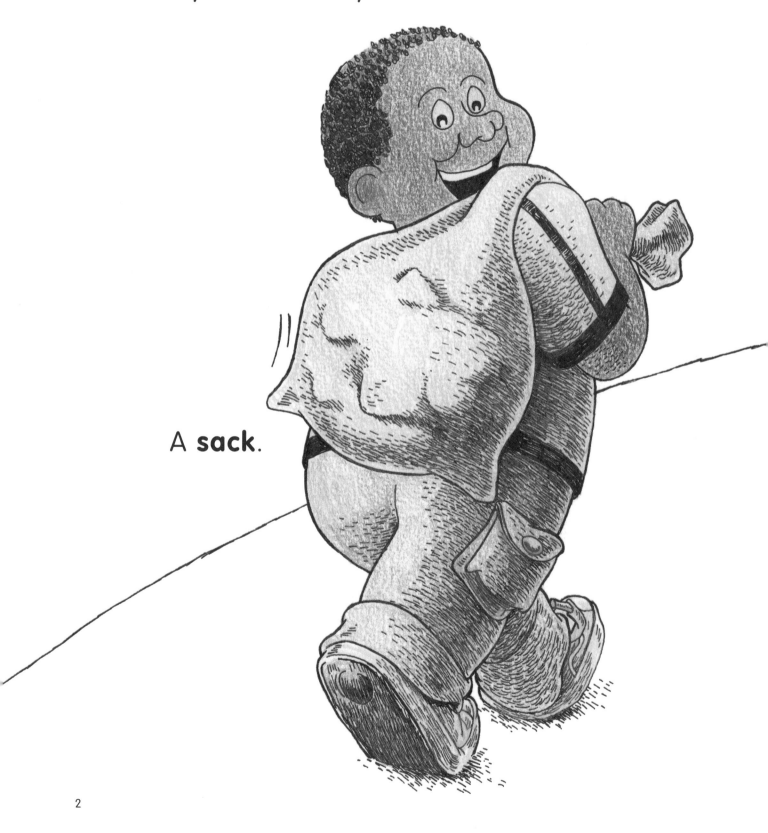

What do you have in your **sack**?

A **snack**.

What do you have in your **room**?

A **broom**.

What do you have in your **house**?

What do you have on your **bed**?

A **mouse**.

Some **bread**.

What do you have
in your **wagon**?

A **dragon**.

What do you have
in your **box**?

A **fox**.

What do you have
on your **chair**?

A **bear**.

8

What do you have on your **stairs**?

More **bears**.

What do you have on your **shirt**?

Some **dirt**.

What do you have in your **gloves**?

Some **doves**.

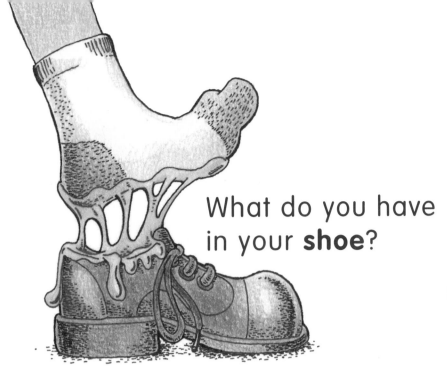

What do you have
in your **shoe**?

Some **glue**.

What do you have
in your **mittens**?

Some **kittens**.

What do you have
on your **lap**?

A **map**.

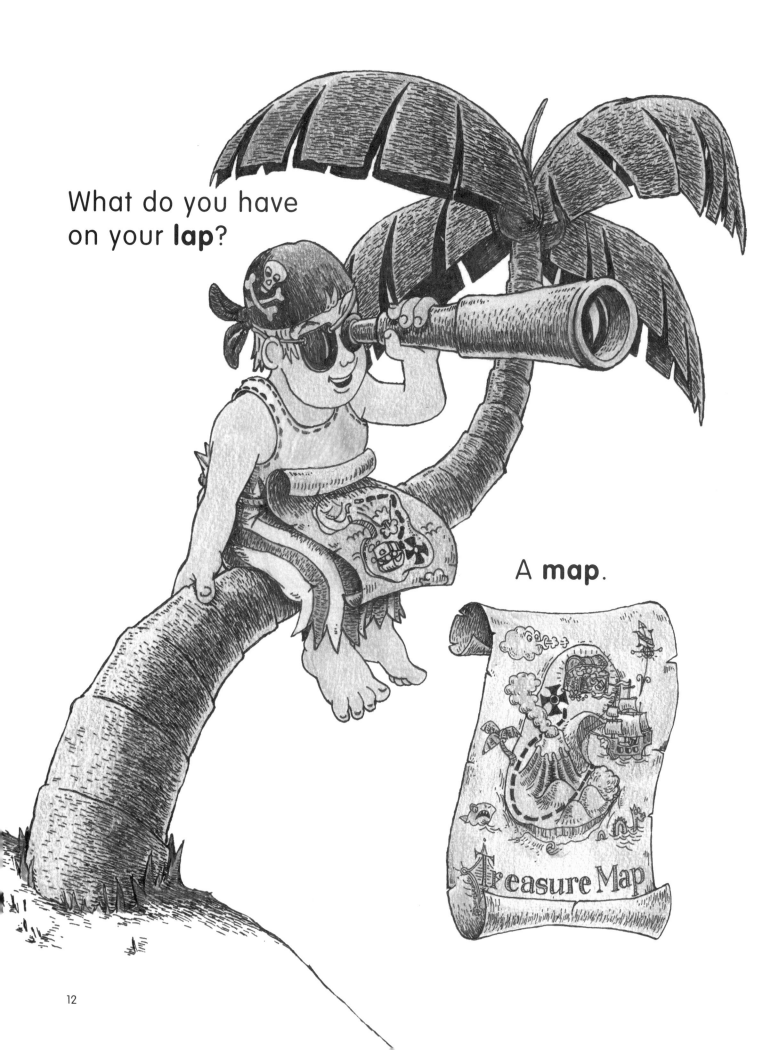

What do you have on your **leg**?

An **egg**.

What do you have on your **chest**?

A **vest**.

What do you have in your **hand**?

Some **sand**.

What do you have on your **shoulder**?

A **boulder**.

What do you have in your **ear**?

A **deer**.

What do you have in your **eye**?

A **pie**.

What do you have
on your **nose**?

A **rose**.

What do you have
in your **hair**?

A **pear**.

21

What do you have in your **socks**?

Some **rocks**.

What do you have in your **bonnet**?

A Book of Sonnets

A **sonnet**.

What do you have in your **cape**?

An **ape**.

What do you have in your **pocket**?

A **locket**.

What do you have in your **coat**?

A **goat**.

What do you have on your **head**?

A **sled**.

What do you have on your **toe**?

A **crow**.

What do you have on your **belly**?

Some **jelly**.

What do you have on
your **knee**?

A **bee**.

What do you have on your **couch**?

A **grouch**.

What do you have
on your **shelf**?

An **elf**.

What do you do with this **book**?

I **look**.